Ashwell: Shadows in the Fog

Catherine J Rosser

Published by Catherine J Rosser, 2024.

This is a work of fiction. Similarities to real people, places, or events are entirely coincidental.

ASHWELL: SHADOWS IN THE FOG

First edition. October 28, 2024.

Copyright © 2024 Catherine J Rosser.

ISBN: 979-8227216632

Written by Catherine J Rosser.

Table of Contents

Ashwell: Shadows in the Fog 1

Chapter One: The Baker's Final Batch 5

Chapter Two: Lou's Last Tune-Up 11

Chapter Three: Maddie's Last Chapter 17

Chapter Four: Father Michael's Final Prayer 23

Chapter Five: Sarah's Last Light 29

Chapter Five: Sarah's Last Light 35

Chapter Six: Echoes of Fear 41

Chapter Seven: The Gathering Shadows 47

Chapter Eight: The Descent 53

Chapter Nine: The Watchful Fog 59

Prologue: Whispers in the Shadows

In the small, hidden town of Ashwell, night has always fallen like a shroud. No stars ever seemed to pierce its black sky. The fog, thick as breath on a windowpane, rolls in over crooked rooftops and narrow, cobblestone streets, pressing against the walls of the weary houses. It's a place that feels damp even in the heat of summer, a place where the ground always smells of moss and rot, and shadows seem to linger a moment too long before melting back into darkness.

No one really remembers how Ashwell came to be. It's just... *there*, as if the mountains that cradle it had one day decided it would be so. Generations had lived and died here, few venturing out, fewer yet venturing in. The place was quaint in its way, isolated in the sort of way that can be romantic on the right night and sinister on every other. When dusk fell, the town was known for going silent as a breath held tight.

Tonight, though, something shifts. The quiet is heavier, almost palpable. The air crackles with a tension that hums in the bones. There's a knowing to it, an expectancy, like a predator crouched low, waiting.

Across the town, lights begin to flicker out. First Edna, at the bakery, blows out her lamp, the light snuffing out like a small gasp. Lou's garage goes dark next, his backdoor slamming shut with a bang that rattles through the narrow streets. Families in their tiny homes lock doors and windows, saying goodnight with hurried words, not lingering too long in any one place. Nobody wants to look out the window. Nobody wants to acknowledge the unspoken rule: when night comes in Ashwell, you don't ask questions.

For the past few nights, a rumor has begun to circulate, like an invisible thread stitching doubt and fear into the fabric of the town. It began as little things, unimportant on their own—a flicker of movement at the edge of vision, shadows where none should be, a strange, hollow laugh that seemed to echo from the woods. But then there was Lou, who'd been found standing on his porch one night, staring out into the darkness, his face pale as milk. When asked what he'd seen, he'd just muttered, "There's something out there," and gone back inside without another word.

The nights grew colder, each one leaving a little something behind—a scrap of fabric caught on a fence, the faint, lingering smell of sulfur, a strange track in the dirt outside of someone's window. And then, last night, someone heard Edna's door open and close... but no one saw her leave.

People in Ashwell are used to their own secrets, the small, private things that make up a life: grudges that have simmered for years, broken promises, whispered gossip. But this is different. This is the kind of secret that makes the air thick and the heart pound too fast. There's something out there, something hiding in the shadows. And it's watching.

Some say it's the mountain spirits, finally rising from their slumber, angry at the town for some forgotten trespass. Others whisper it's a ghost, or worse—a demon, born of the town's collective sins, here to collect its due. And some, those who've seen the strange shadows moving through the streets at night, are convinced it's a killer, lurking just out of sight.

But what they all know, even if they won't say it out loud, is that whatever this *thing* is, it's come to Ashwell for a reason.

Tonight, as the last light in town goes out and the fog thickens, curling around houses and alleyways like a lover's embrace, a chill settles over Ashwell, a breath held too long in the darkness. The people lock their doors and pull their curtains tight, whispering prayers to whoever might listen. They know they won't sleep well tonight. They know that tomorrow, someone else might be gone.

As the clock strikes midnight, a single scream cuts through the fog, slicing the night open like a wound. It's followed by silence, a hollow, suffocating silence that drapes over the town like a burial shroud.

And just beyond the reach of the town's faint, flickering lights, something waits, grinning in the darkness.

Chapter One: The Baker's Final Batch

Morning dawned in Ashwell, though dawn was a loose term here, where the sun was more suggestion than reality. A thin, pale light sifted through the fog, brushing over rooftops and half-heartedly touching the streets. Ashwell's residents woke to the slow, gray crawl of another day, stretching limbs and rubbing the chill from their faces, each one holding their breath a second longer than usual before getting out of bed. Just in case.

Edna was already at work by the time the rest of the town started to rouse. She was a woman of routine, rising each morning before the rooster's crow, before the town had even blinked itself awake. Her bakery, a tiny squat building that had seen better days, smelled of warm bread, sweet rolls, and the occasional tart if she was feeling generous. She could be prickly, sure, but her pastries were nothing short of divine, and no one dared to criticize a woman who held the town's carb supply in her flour-dusted hands.

But this morning felt different.

As she rolled out dough on her wooden counter, hands moving with a practiced rhythm, she couldn't shake a prickling sensation at the back of her neck. It was as though someone—or something—was watching her, eyes tracking her every move from just beyond the edge of her vision. She glanced up at the small window over the sink, squinting into the fog, which seemed thicker than usual, pressing against the glass like it wanted to seep inside.

"Edna, don't be daft," she muttered to herself, shaking off the feeling with a huff. She returned to her work, kneading the dough with a fierceness that betrayed more than just the annoyance of an aging baker's aching hands.

Still, she couldn't shake it. The feeling clung to her, slipping around her like the scent of yeast in the air. The small noises of her kitchen—the clinking of bowls, the scrape of metal against wood—seemed muted, as though swallowed by some invisible maw. The silence outside was worse. No birds. No rustling wind. Just the eerie, unnatural stillness that had draped itself over Ashwell for days.

Then came the knock.

It was barely audible, a soft tap-tap-tap that would have been lost if she hadn't been listening so intently. Her hands froze mid-knead, and she tilted her head, brow furrowing as she strained to hear it again. Tap-tap-tap. Three knocks, each one softer than the last, like fingers barely brushing the wood.

"Who in blazes would be knocking this early?" she grumbled. Her eyes darted to the clock on the wall, where the minute hand crept toward five. Too early for customers, even for the likes of Lou, who usually ambled in just after sunrise for his morning bread.

Heart pounding in her chest, she wiped her hands on her apron, moving slowly toward the door, each step heavy with the reluctance of someone who knew—*just knew*—that something wasn't right. She hesitated with her hand on the knob, cursing herself for the irrational fear creeping through her. But fear or not, curiosity won out.

The door swung open with a creak, the fog rolling in like an uninvited guest, curling around her ankles. She squinted into the thick, gray soup beyond her doorstep, straining to make out any shape, any sign of the knocker.

Nothing.

"Who's there?" she called, her voice rough but steady. Silence answered her, a thick, heavy kind that seemed to smother her words before they even reached the edge of the porch. Her stomach twisted, her instincts screaming at her to slam the door and bolt it, but her pride kept her rooted in place.

Then, just as she was about to step back inside, she saw it—a faint outline in the fog, barely visible, a shape that seemed to waver and shift, like smoke trapped in a jar. She couldn't make out a face, just a suggestion of form, something tall and lean, with limbs that seemed too long, stretching out in ways that defied logic.

"Is... is someone there?" she whispered, her voice barely a breath.

The shape didn't move, didn't respond. It simply hovered there, watching her with an intensity that made her skin crawl. And then, with a slow, almost lazy motion, it raised one elongated arm, fingers unfurling like the petals of a dead flower, and pointed directly at her.

Something snapped in her—a primal instinct, a scream clawing its way up her throat, though no sound came out. She stumbled back, slamming the door and bolting it, pressing her weight against the wood as if that would somehow keep whatever that thing was on the other side.

Heart hammering, she stood there, breath coming in short, shallow gasps, her hand pressed to her chest as if trying to steady the frantic beat. Her mind raced, trying to rationalize what she'd just seen, to dismiss it as some trick of the fog, her own overworked imagination. But deep down, she knew. That wasn't her imagination. It was real, and it was here, right on her doorstep.

The rest of the morning passed in a blur. She went through the motions of baking, kneading dough and shaping rolls, her hands moving on autopilot while her mind remained fixed on that shape in the fog, that impossible figure with its accusing finger.

And then, just before opening time, she heard it again. Tap-tap-tap. Her body went cold, her muscles locking in place as she listened, her breath shallow and trembling.

This time, she didn't go to the door. She stayed rooted behind the counter, her eyes locked on the doorway, waiting, listening. The knock came again, a little louder, a little more insistent. Tap-tap-tap. Her hands shook, fingers gripping the edge of the counter so tightly her knuckles turned white.

She tried to tell herself it was nothing, just a trick of the wind, or maybe Lou playing a prank. But deep down, she knew better. The fear that gripped her was raw, primal, and utterly inescapable.

And then, just as quickly as it had come, the knocking stopped. The silence returned, thick and heavy, wrapping around her like a noose. She waited, heart pounding, every nerve in her body on edge, but no other sound came.

Finally, after what felt like an eternity, she dared to step away from the counter, her footsteps slow and cautious. She moved to the window, peering out into the fog, searching for any sign of that shape, that figure that had haunted her doorstep. But the street was empty, the fog dense and impenetrable.

For a moment, she allowed herself to breathe, to relax, her shoulders sagging with the weight of her relief.

And then, just as she turned away from the window, she caught a glimpse of it—the faintest outline of a handprint on the glass, smeared and elongated, like fingers stretching out from some forgotten nightmare.

The scream that finally tore from her throat was raw, ripping through the silence of the bakery, echoing down the empty streets. By the time anyone arrived, Edna was gone. The door was ajar, the scent of fresh bread wafting through the air, and on the counter lay a single, cold loaf, her final batch, untouched and waiting.

No one would ever see Edna again. But the mark she left—the terror, the whispers—would linger, a stain on the town's collective memory, the beginning of something none of them were prepared to face.

Chapter Two: Lou's Last Tune-Up

The morning after Edna's disappearance, Ashwell awoke to an uneasy stillness. The bakery remained dark, its windows bare and lifeless. Usually, by dawn, the scent of bread would fill the street, the warm aroma drifting into Lou's garage across the road. Today, there was only the sour chill of morning air, laced with fog that hugged the ground like a veil.

Lou had noticed. He wasn't the type to fret—"worry ages a man," he'd always say—but Edna's absence gnawed at him. She was as predictable as sunrise. He figured she was just running late, though he couldn't recall a time that had happened before.

As he rolled up the sleeves of his oil-stained shirt, Lou tried to shake the uneasy feeling that had settled over him like a second skin. He was a simple man—tools and metal, grease and gasoline. He knew engines better than people. But this... this was different. He could feel it, creeping under his skin, a whisper of dread that made the hairs on his arms stand on end. And there was that strange knocking he'd heard outside his window last night, three sharp taps that had echoed in his chest. When he looked outside, there was no one there. Just the fog, thick and silent, pressing against his window.

Still, work was work, and Lou had a reputation to uphold. He flipped on the lights of his garage, casting a yellow glow over the rows of tools, the half-dismantled engine on his workbench, and the walls lined with photos of his younger years, back when his hair wasn't gray and his hands didn't ache in the mornings. He fiddled with the radio until it crackled to life, filling the space with a scratchy rendition of an old blues tune. It was familiar, grounding.

Hours passed. Lou worked, his hands moving automatically as his mind drifted, replaying the night's eerie events in an endless loop. The way the fog had seemed to pulse, alive and watchful. The shadow he'd seen flicker in the alleyway as he'd walked home from the pub. The sound of footsteps that had echoed his own, just half a beat behind, until he'd reached his front door. Even then, he'd felt a strange pull, a need to look back, as though something—*someone*—was right there, waiting. But he hadn't dared. Instead, he'd locked his door, poured a glass of bourbon, and tried to chase away the fear that gnawed at him like rust on metal.

Just as he was settling into a rhythm, there was a sound. A low, shuffling noise that echoed through the quiet garage. He looked up, expecting to see a customer. But the doorway was empty.

"Hello?" he called out, his voice rough but steady.

Nothing.

He shrugged it off, convincing himself it was his imagination, or maybe a raccoon scrounging around outside. But a minute later, it came again—a soft, scraping sound, like something being dragged across the floor. He frowned, setting down his wrench, and wiped his hands on a rag as he moved cautiously toward the back of the garage, where the sound seemed to originate.

The light back there was dim, barely illuminating the shadows that seemed to stretch and curl along the walls. The smell of gasoline was thick, familiar, comforting in its own way. But beneath it was something else—a faint, rancid odor, something sour and metallic, like blood and rust.

"Alright, enough games," he muttered, forcing his voice to sound braver than he felt. "Whoever's in here, you better show yourself, or I'll call the sheriff."

Silence.

He took another step forward, his boots echoing on the concrete floor. And then, out of the corner of his eye, he saw it—a flash of movement, a quick, skittering shadow that darted across the wall, there one moment and gone the next.

Lou's heart stuttered, and he gripped the wrench tighter, his knuckles turning white. He swallowed hard, his mouth dry as sandpaper. He wasn't a man easily frightened, but there was something deeply wrong here, something that sent ice sliding down his spine.

"Alright," he whispered, more to himself than anyone else. "Get a grip, Lou. It's just a shadow, just your mind playing tricks."

But even as he said it, he didn't believe it. The air felt thick, suffocating, pressing against his chest like a weight. He turned to head back to his workbench, his steps quicker now, a desperate urge to put distance between himself and that dark corner.

And then, he heard it. The knocking. Three sharp, deliberate knocks, echoing through the garage, louder this time, like a fist pounding against the metal walls.

He froze, every muscle in his body going rigid. The knocking came again, insistent, demanding, as though whatever was out there wanted him to come closer.

Against his better judgment, he turned toward the sound. He could feel his heartbeat drumming in his ears, each beat heavy and thick. The knocking continued, each knock louder than the last, echoing through the silent garage, reverberating off the walls until it felt like it was coming from inside his own skull.

And then, just as suddenly as it had started, it stopped. Silence filled the space, thick and oppressive, pressing down on him like a hand around his throat. He stood there, frozen, his hand still gripping the wrench, his eyes fixed on the shadows that seemed to shift and dance in the dim light.

A part of him knew he should turn back, go outside, call for help. But something held him in place, a strange, irresistible pull that tugged at him, drawing him forward, deeper into the darkness.

He took a step, then another, his feet moving almost of their own accord. The shadows seemed to swell, wrapping around him, filling his vision until all he could see was darkness. He reached out, his fingers brushing against something cold and damp, the smell of rot filling his nostrils.

And then, he felt it—a hand, thin and bony, wrapping around his wrist with a grip like iron. He tried to pull back, but the hand held him fast, its fingers digging into his skin with an unnatural strength.

Panic surged through him, his heart pounding as he struggled against the unseen force. He opened his mouth to scream, but no sound came out. The darkness seemed to press in on him, swallowing his breath, his voice, his very sense of self.

And then, in the faint light filtering in from the front of the garage, he saw it—a face, pale and twisted, its eyes black pits that seemed to stare straight through him. A mouth stretched wide in a grotesque smile, lips pulled back to reveal jagged, yellowed teeth. It leaned in close, its breath cold and rancid against his skin, and whispered his name in a voice that sounded like dead leaves scraping across stone.

"Lou..."

In that moment, he knew he was lost, his fate sealed. He could feel the life draining out of him, his strength ebbing away, his vision blurring as the darkness closed in around him.

The last thing he saw was that face, grinning down at him with a sickening, hungry gleam in its eyes, as though savoring his fear, feeding off his terror.

And then, there was nothing.

The garage was silent, the air heavy with the lingering scent of gasoline and decay. Lou's workbench was untouched, his tools neatly lined up as always. But he was gone. All that remained was a faint smear of blood on the concrete floor, and the faint, lingering echo of his name whispered in the darkness.

Chapter Three:
Maddie's Last
Chapter

The morning fog drifted lazily past the tall windows of Ashwell's library, wrapping the stone building in a veil of gray. Inside, the quiet was almost sacred, broken only by the occasional rustle of pages and the ticking of the old clock mounted above the door. The library was Maddie's haven, her refuge from a world that often felt too loud, too fast. Here, in the soft glow of warm lamps and surrounded by shelves groaning under the weight of old stories and forgotten histories, she felt safe. Or at least, she *used* to.

Today, though, that familiar comfort was gone. The silence didn't feel welcoming—it felt watchful, a hush that pressed against her eardrums, thick and smothering. Her usual morning routine—re-shelving books, dusting, straightening chairs—felt more like an exercise in distraction. She couldn't shake the nagging sensation that something was wrong, a prickling unease that crawled under her skin like tiny spiders.

The news of Edna and Lou's disappearances had spread through the town like wildfire. People were murmuring about it everywhere—in the market, outside the church, even on the rare phone calls that managed to get through the increasingly unreliable lines. There was no sign of Edna or Lou, just a few scattered clues: bloodstains, broken glass, a single handprint smeared on Edna's bakery window. It was as though the town itself had swallowed them whole.

Maddie tried to push the thought aside, forcing herself to focus on her tasks. She picked up a stack of returns, clutching them against her chest like a shield as she walked down one of the narrow aisles. The shelves loomed around her, tall and dark, casting long shadows that seemed to shift and twist as she moved. The dim lighting didn't help; it left half the library cloaked in shadow, and for the first time, she found herself wishing she wasn't alone.

She turned the corner and froze, her heart skipping a beat. A book lay open on the floor, its pages splayed out like the wings of a dead bird. Maddie frowned; she was meticulous about keeping the library tidy. She knelt down, hesitating just a moment before reaching for the book. The title was faded, the cover worn, and when she brushed her fingers across it, a chill ran through her. The book felt cold, unnaturally so, as though it had been left outside in the dead of winter.

The title read *Dark Reflections*, a dusty tome she hadn't seen anyone check out in years. It was a collection of old folktales, eerie stories passed down from Ashwell's earliest days, back when the town had been little more than a cluster of cabins huddled against the mountains. Her fingers trembled slightly as she closed the book, her reflection glinting faintly in the cracked glass of an old picture frame on the wall. In the dim light, she thought she saw something move behind her—a shadow shifting, a fleeting glimpse of something that didn't belong.

She stood up quickly, clutching the book to her chest, her breath coming in short, shallow gasps. She felt silly, childish, but the fear was real, coiling in her stomach like a living thing. She tried to shake it off, laughing nervously to herself.

"Get a grip, Maddie. It's just a book. It's only a story," she whispered, her voice barely louder than a breath.

The library seemed to respond, the silence growing deeper, more oppressive. She forced herself to walk back to the front desk, her footsteps echoing unnaturally loud in the stillness. She tried to ignore the creeping sensation that someone was watching her, that if she turned around, she'd see a face staring back at her from the shadows.

She placed the book on the desk, her hands trembling as she reached for the logbook to make a note. But as she opened the log, her pen hovered in midair, frozen. The date was already written in neat, precise handwriting—her own handwriting. Next to it, in dark, spidery letters, were the words: *Maddie's Last Chapter.*

She stared at the words, her mind stumbling over the impossible sight. She hadn't written that. She would remember. And yet, there it was, as clear as the fear gnawing at her heart. Her hands went cold, the chill spreading through her chest as she tried to understand.

A noise broke the silence—a faint whisper, barely more than a sigh, drifting through the empty library. It was impossible to tell where it came from; it seemed to seep from the walls themselves, wrapping around her in a low, insistent murmur. She couldn't make out the words, but the tone was unmistakable: hungry, eager, like something savoring a final meal.

"Maddie..."

Her name echoed softly through the room, the voice slow and lingering, stretching the syllables as if tasting each one. She whipped around, her heart hammering against her ribs, her eyes scanning the shadows that filled every corner. She saw nothing—only rows of books, silent and indifferent. But the voice lingered, wrapping around her like a cold embrace.

Her first instinct was to run. Her legs tensed, ready to bolt, but something held her in place. The same strange, compelling force that had made her pick up the book, that had drawn her toward the library this morning despite the gnawing sense of dread that had settled over her the moment she'd woken up.

Taking a shaky breath, she took a step forward, her eyes locked on the dark aisle at the far end of the library. The shadows seemed to deepen as she approached, swallowing the weak light that filtered in through the windows. The air grew colder, the rancid smell of damp and decay filling her nostrils, and she had to suppress a gag as she forced herself to keep walking.

Her footsteps echoed, too loud, each step a challenge to the silence that seemed to throb with its own life. She could feel her pulse pounding in her temples, her breath hitching with each beat. And then, just as she reached the end of the aisle, she saw it—a figure, barely visible, lurking in the shadows.

It was tall and thin, its limbs impossibly long, its face hidden in darkness. But she could see its eyes—two gleaming, black pits that seemed to swallow the light, staring at her with a hunger that made her skin crawl. It raised one hand, bony fingers stretching out toward her, beckoning.

"Who... who are you?" Maddie's voice was barely a whisper, each word trembling on her lips.

The figure didn't answer. It just stood there, silent and still, its eyes fixed on her, watching her with a strange, predatory patience. And then, slowly, it began to move, gliding forward, its steps silent, smooth as a shadow sliding across the floor.

Maddie backed away, her mind screaming at her to run, but her body felt frozen, paralyzed by the terror that gripped her. She stumbled, her back hitting the bookshelf behind her, sending a cascade of books tumbling to the floor. The figure didn't stop, didn't pause, its gaze never wavering.

Desperation flooded her, and she reached blindly behind her, grabbing a book at random, her fingers clutching it like a lifeline. She hurled it toward the figure, her voice breaking in a scream that echoed through the empty library.

But the figure only paused, tilting its head as if amused, watching as the book fell harmlessly to the floor. Its lips curved in a smile, a grotesque, hungry grin that stretched too wide, showing teeth that gleamed like polished bone.

And then, before she could react, it was upon her, its cold hands wrapping around her wrists, its face inches from her own. The stench of rot filled her nose, making her gag as she struggled against its grip, but it held her fast, its strength inhuman, unyielding.

It leaned closer, its breath cold and rancid against her cheek, and whispered in her ear, its voice low and mocking.

"This is where your story ends, Maddie."

In that final, horrifying moment, she saw her reflection in its eyes, twisted and distorted, her face a mask of terror. And then the darkness closed in, swallowing her whole, leaving only the echo of her final scream lingering in the empty library.

The librarian's desk was empty, a single book lying open on its surface. *Dark Reflections,* its pages spread wide, as though welcoming someone to read. The words "Maddie's Last Chapter" were scrawled across the top of the page in dark, jagged letters, the ink smeared, as if written by a trembling hand.

And Ashwell's library was silent once more.

Chapter Four: Father Michael's Final Prayer

The morning after Maddie's disappearance, the church in Ashwell sat as still as the fog that wrapped itself around the town like a shroud. Inside, the sanctuary was dim, shafts of light streaming through stained glass windows to cast fractured colors onto the stone walls. It was cold, colder than usual, and the air held the heavy scent of wax and incense, mingling with an unshakable dampness that clung to the pews and floor.

Father Michael moved slowly down the aisle, his footsteps muffled by the thick, worn carpet. He was no stranger to the weight of silence, but today it felt different. *Heavier.* Ashwell had always been a quiet town, but now the quiet had taken on a sinister edge, an absence that felt like it was waiting to be filled.

He had tried to keep his congregation calm, offering words of hope and comfort in the wake of Edna's, Lou's, and Maddie's disappearances, but his own spirit was growing weary. Each night, he prayed for guidance, for protection over his small flock, but with each prayer came a creeping dread, a feeling that his words were falling into an abyss, swallowed by something darker than doubt.

Father Michael was a man of faith, unwavering even in the face of the town's whispers about curses and restless spirits. But he wasn't blind. He could feel it—an unseen presence lurking at the edges of his vision, a shadow that seemed to follow him, lingering in the corners of the church, where the light didn't quite reach.

He'd first noticed it last night, after the last of his parishioners had left, and he'd stayed behind to extinguish the candles. The flames had flickered, the shadows casting strange, shifting shapes on the walls, and he could have sworn he heard footsteps echoing softly behind him. But when he'd turned, the church had been empty, silent as a tomb.

Today, as he prepared for the morning's service, the feeling was worse. He couldn't shake the sensation that he was being watched, that every movement was monitored by unseen eyes. He tried to ignore it, focusing on his duties, preparing the altar, setting the chalice, arranging the cloth. But each movement felt labored, his hands trembling slightly as he placed the chalice on the altar.

The whispers started faintly, so quiet he almost thought they were a figment of his mind, lingering at the edge of hearing. A soft murmur, like the rustling of leaves in a distant forest, only there was no wind, no sound other than his own breathing.

As he began to light the candles, the whispers grew louder, taking on a strange cadence, a rhythm that seemed to seep into his bones. He strained to catch the words, but they were foreign, a guttural language that scraped across his nerves like nails on a chalkboard.

"Who's there?" he called out, his voice echoing through the empty sanctuary. His own voice sounded small, swallowed by the dark corners of the room. Silence answered him, the whispers cutting off abruptly, leaving the space hollow and tense.

With a deep breath, he forced himself to continue with the preparations. But his hands were trembling now, the matches slipping from his grasp and clattering onto the altar. He leaned against the altar for support, closing his eyes and murmuring a prayer under his breath, trying to steady himself. He could feel his heart pounding, each beat like a drum echoing through the stillness.

And then, behind him, a shadow shifted.

He sensed it before he saw it, the prickle of awareness crawling up his spine. He turned slowly, his eyes scanning the empty pews, the shadows stretching long and dark in the dim light. Nothing moved, but the air felt colder, and the silence had taken on a weight, a presence that pressed down on him like a vice.

He opened his mouth to speak, but the words died on his tongue. In the far corner of the sanctuary, just at the edge of his vision, a figure stood. It was cloaked in shadow, its form indistinct, blending with the darkness like ink spilled into water. But he could make out the eyes—two gleaming points of light, watching him with an intensity that sent a shiver through his soul.

"Who... who are you?" he whispered, his voice barely more than a breath.

The figure didn't move, didn't respond. It simply watched him, its eyes gleaming with a strange, predatory hunger. The silence stretched, thick and oppressive, as though the very walls were closing in around him.

He took a step back, his heart pounding, his fingers gripping the edge of the altar as though it were an anchor in a storm. The whispers started again, louder this time, filling the space with their guttural, nonsensical murmur. He couldn't understand the words, but he could feel the malice behind them, the cold, creeping hatred that seeped into his bones, chilling him to the core.

Summoning every ounce of courage, he raised his hand, forming the sign of the cross. His voice shook as he spoke, but he forced the words out, each syllable a lifeline.

"In the name of the Father, the Son, and the Holy—"

Before he could finish, the candles on the altar flickered, their flames dimming, then snuffing out one by one. Darkness flooded the sanctuary, swallowing the light, leaving him standing in the pitch-black, alone with the whispers and the thing in the shadows.

He could feel it moving closer, the air growing colder with each step it took, pressing against him like a suffocating weight. His breath came in shallow gasps, his mind racing, desperation clawing at his heart. He tried to pray, to call upon his faith, but the words felt hollow, empty, dissolving in the thick darkness that pressed in around him.

The figure drew closer, its face now visible in the dim light that filtered through the stained glass. It was pale, almost skeletal, its skin stretched tight over sharp bones, its mouth curved in a grotesque, mocking smile. Its eyes gleamed with a sickly light, hollow and hungry, devouring him with their gaze.

"Faith will not save you," it whispered, its voice a low, rasping hiss that scraped against his nerves. The words echoed in his mind, twisting his thoughts, filling him with a terror so profound it left him paralyzed.

He tried to speak, to scream, but no sound came out. The darkness pressed in, filling his lungs, suffocating him, as though it were alive, pulsing and shifting around him, a living shadow that wrapped him in its cold embrace.

The figure reached out, its hand skeletal, its fingers long and sharp, like claws. It touched his forehead, a cold, searing pressure that sent pain lancing through his skull. He felt his strength draining, his vision blurring as the darkness seeped into him, filling him, consuming him.

His last thought was a desperate, silent prayer, a plea for mercy, for salvation. But there was no answer. Only the darkness, swallowing him whole, leaving nothing but an empty silence where he had once stood.

The church was empty, the sanctuary dark and cold. The parishioners who arrived for the morning service found the altar bare, the candles unlit, the air heavy with the lingering scent of incense and something else—something faintly metallic, like blood.

Father Michael was gone, leaving only a Bible open on the altar, the pages smudged and torn, the words barely legible. A single phrase was scrawled across the page in dark, jagged letters, as though written in haste, or perhaps desperation:

"There is no salvation here."

And the church, like the rest of Ashwell, fell silent once more.

Chapter Five: Sarah's Last Light

The farmhouse at the edge of Ashwell had seen better days. Sarah Monroe had inherited it from her grandmother, a sturdy but aging building with creaking floors, drafty windows, and a peculiar charm that Sarah found comforting. The house was her haven, perched at the edge of town with nothing but forest stretching out behind it. She was grateful for the seclusion—until now.

As dusk settled over the town, casting long shadows across the fields, Sarah felt an unfamiliar chill settle in her bones. She wrapped a woolen shawl around her shoulders, peering out the window at the creeping fog that seemed to grow thicker each night, swallowing the edges of her yard, wrapping around the trunks of the trees like a hungry specter. She'd heard the stories—Edna, Lou, Maddie, Father Michael—all vanished without a trace. Only unsettling fragments left behind, like breadcrumbs leading into a nightmare.

Sarah wasn't one for ghost stories or superstition. But after four disappearances, even she couldn't ignore the unease that hung over Ashwell like a storm cloud. She'd taken to bolting her doors, lighting candles in every room, as if the warm light might somehow keep the darkness at bay. Tonight, she'd drawn the curtains tightly over every window, leaving only a small sliver open in the kitchen. She couldn't explain why, but she felt better being able to watch the fog, as if she could somehow see danger coming if she kept an eye on it.

The farmhouse was silent, save for the crackling of the fire and the ticking of the clock on the mantle. The quiet didn't feel like peace tonight; it felt like waiting, a pause before something terrible. She moved from room to room, lighting lamps and muttering under her breath. It was silly, she knew, but there was something comforting in the little rituals, the simple acts of illumination.

As she reached the last room, a small storage closet just off the kitchen, a knock echoed through the house—a single, sharp rap that seemed to vibrate in the silence. She froze, her breath hitching, her mind racing. She hadn't been expecting anyone, especially not at this hour.

"Who's there?" she called out, her voice steady despite the pounding in her chest.

No response.

A second knock came, louder this time, more insistent. It was coming from the front door, a door she'd bolted and latched with the heaviest lock she could find. She moved slowly, her bare feet whispering across the wooden floor, her body tense, every muscle ready to flee. Her fingers tightened around the handle of the cast-iron skillet she'd been using to cook, holding it like a makeshift weapon.

"Who is it?" she called again, her voice sharper this time, a desperate edge to her tone.

The silence that followed was thick, almost tangible, pressing against her eardrums. She took another step forward, her eyes fixed on the front door, her mind caught in a tug-of-war between fear and curiosity. Finally, unable to bear it any longer, she reached out and flipped the latch.

As the door creaked open, the fog seemed to spill in like water, thick and swirling, curling around her feet. She squinted into the mist, her heart racing as she searched for any sign of a person, an animal—anything that could explain the knocking. But the porch was empty, the yard stretching out into the dark, silent and still.

She was about to close the door when she saw it: a figure standing at the edge of her property, just beyond the fence. It was little more than a shadow in the fog, a shape that seemed to shift and flicker, as though it were both there and not there at the same time.

"Hello?" she called out, her voice barely more than a whisper.

The figure didn't move, didn't respond. It simply stood there, watching her, a silent sentinel cloaked in darkness. The fog thickened around it, obscuring its features, but she could make out the faint gleam of eyes, two pinpoints of light that seemed to pierce through the mist, locking onto her with an intensity that sent a shiver down her spine.

She felt her breath hitch, a primal, gut-wrenching fear clawing its way up her throat. But she couldn't look away, couldn't tear her gaze from those eyes. They were hollow, empty, yet filled with a strange, unnatural hunger, as if the thing behind them was savoring her terror, feeding off it.

Slowly, the figure raised one hand, a thin, bony limb that seemed to stretch impossibly long, fingers curling like talons. It pointed directly at her, its mouth twisting into a grotesque grin that sent a fresh wave of fear through her. Her hands began to shake, her grip on the skillet loosening as her mind screamed at her to run, to lock herself away and never look back.

But as she took a step back, the figure moved, gliding forward, its steps silent, each one bringing it closer to the porch, to her. She stumbled backward, slamming the door shut and bolting it with trembling hands, her breath coming in shallow gasps. She pressed her back against the door, her heart pounding, the cold metal of the skillet clutched to her chest like a shield.

For a moment, there was only silence, the thick, suffocating quiet that filled the house like a fog. And then, the knocking began again—louder this time, as though something were pounding on the wood with a strength that defied human limits. The door rattled, the wood creaking under the force, and she could feel the vibrations reverberating through her bones.

"Go away!" she screamed, her voice breaking, but the knocking didn't stop. It grew louder, faster, until it was a relentless hammering that filled her mind, drowning out every thought, every instinct but one: survive.

She ran to the kitchen, grabbing her lantern from the counter, the warm glow flickering as she held it up like a lifeline. She backed toward the cellar door, her mind racing, searching for a way out, a place to hide. The cellar had a small, hidden hatch that led out to the forest; if she could just reach it, maybe she could escape, lose herself in the trees until whatever was outside gave up.

But as she fumbled with the lock, trying to pry it open, the pounding stopped. Silence fell once more, heavy and unnatural, as though the house were holding its breath. She turned slowly, the lantern trembling in her hands as she peered back toward the front door.

The figure was inside.

It stood in the doorway, its tall, thin form framed by the faint light of the moon filtering through the curtains. Its face was a mask of shadows, its eyes gleaming with that same unholy light, its mouth twisted into a grotesque, toothy smile. It took a step forward, its movements slow, deliberate, as though savoring the horror etched across her face.

Sarah felt her legs weaken, her body refusing to obey her commands, paralyzed by the sheer, overwhelming terror that gripped her. She stumbled back, her hand finding the cold, rough surface of the cellar door, her last hope slipping through her fingers as the figure moved closer.

In a final, desperate act, she raised the lantern, hurling it at the thing with all her strength. The glass shattered, flames bursting to life, casting eerie shadows across the room. For a moment, she thought she saw it flinch, its form twisting in the firelight, its face contorting with something that almost looked like anger.

But then, it stepped through the flames, unscathed, its eyes gleaming with a hungry, malevolent light. It was close now, so close she could feel its icy breath on her skin, smell the rancid stench of decay that clung to it like a second skin.

"Sarah..." it whispered, its voice a low, mocking hiss that sent chills down her spine. "There's no escaping me."

In a final, instinctive burst of fear, she turned, wrenching the cellar door open and stumbling down the stairs. She could hear it behind her, its footsteps slow but relentless, each one echoing in the small space like the tolling of a death bell.

She reached the bottom, her fingers scrabbling at the edge of the hatch. But as she lifted it, something cold wrapped around her ankle, yanking her back with a strength that sent her sprawling to the floor. She screamed, her voice echoing off the stone walls, but there was no one to hear her, no one to save her.

The last thing she saw was its face, twisted into a smile of pure malice, its eyes gleaming with satisfaction as it dragged her into the darkness. The light from the flames above flickered, casting shadows across the walls, but soon even that faded, leaving only the cold, silent dark.

The next morning, the farmhouse was empty. The front door hung open, the kitchen cold and lifeless. Only a faint trail of scorched wood led from the front door to the cellar, ending abruptly in a smudge of ash and the faint, lingering scent of smoke.

Ashwell fell silent once more, the fog thicker than ever, curling around the town like a predator licking its lips. And another house stood empty, another life swallowed by the shadows.

Chapter Five: Sarah's Last Light

The farmhouse at the edge of Ashwell had seen better days. Sarah Monroe had inherited it from her grandmother, a sturdy but aging building with creaking floors, drafty windows, and a peculiar charm that Sarah found comforting. The house was her haven, perched at the edge of town with nothing but forest stretching out behind it. She was grateful for the seclusion—until now.

As dusk settled over the town, casting long shadows across the fields, Sarah felt an unfamiliar chill settle in her bones. She wrapped a woolen shawl around her shoulders, peering out the window at the creeping fog that seemed to grow thicker each night, swallowing the edges of her yard, wrapping around the trunks of the trees like a hungry specter. She'd heard the stories—Edna, Lou, Maddie, Father Michael—all vanished without a trace. Only unsettling fragments left behind, like breadcrumbs leading into a nightmare.

Sarah wasn't one for ghost stories or superstition. But after four disappearances, even she couldn't ignore the unease that hung over Ashwell like a storm cloud. She'd taken to bolting her doors, lighting candles in every room, as if the warm light might somehow keep the darkness at bay. Tonight, she'd drawn the curtains tightly over every window, leaving only a small sliver open in the kitchen. She couldn't explain why, but she felt better being able to watch the fog, as if she could somehow see danger coming if she kept an eye on it.

The farmhouse was silent, save for the crackling of the fire and the ticking of the clock on the mantle. The quiet didn't feel like peace tonight; it felt like waiting, a pause before something terrible. She moved from room to room, lighting lamps and muttering under her breath. It was silly, she knew, but there was something comforting in the little rituals, the simple acts of illumination.

As she reached the last room, a small storage closet just off the kitchen, a knock echoed through the house—a single, sharp rap that seemed to vibrate in the silence. She froze, her breath hitching, her mind racing. She hadn't been expecting anyone, especially not at this hour.

"Who's there?" she called out, her voice steady despite the pounding in her chest.

No response.

A second knock came, louder this time, more insistent. It was coming from the front door, a door she'd bolted and latched with the heaviest lock she could find. She moved slowly, her bare feet whispering across the wooden floor, her body tense, every muscle ready to flee. Her fingers tightened around the handle of the cast-iron skillet she'd been using to cook, holding it like a makeshift weapon.

"Who is it?" she called again, her voice sharper this time, a desperate edge to her tone.

The silence that followed was thick, almost tangible, pressing against her eardrums. She took another step forward, her eyes fixed on the front door, her mind caught in a tug-of-war between fear and curiosity. Finally, unable to bear it any longer, she reached out and flipped the latch.

As the door creaked open, the fog seemed to spill in like water, thick and swirling, curling around her feet. She squinted into the mist, her heart racing as she searched for any sign of a person, an animal—anything that could explain the knocking. But the porch was empty, the yard stretching out into the dark, silent and still.

She was about to close the door when she saw it: a figure standing at the edge of her property, just beyond the fence. It was little more than a shadow in the fog, a shape that seemed to shift and flicker, as though it were both there and not there at the same time.

"Hello?" she called out, her voice barely more than a whisper.

The figure didn't move, didn't respond. It simply stood there, watching her, a silent sentinel cloaked in darkness. The fog thickened around it, obscuring its features, but she could make out the faint gleam of eyes, two pinpoints of light that seemed to pierce through the mist, locking onto her with an intensity that sent a shiver down her spine.

She felt her breath hitch, a primal, gut-wrenching fear clawing its way up her throat. But she couldn't look away, couldn't tear her gaze from those eyes. They were hollow, empty, yet filled with a strange, unnatural hunger, as if the thing behind them was savoring her terror, feeding off it.

Slowly, the figure raised one hand, a thin, bony limb that seemed to stretch impossibly long, fingers curling like talons. It pointed directly at her, its mouth twisting into a grotesque grin that sent a fresh wave of fear through her. Her hands began to shake, her grip on the skillet loosening as her mind screamed at her to run, to lock herself away and never look back.

But as she took a step back, the figure moved, gliding forward, its steps silent, each one bringing it closer to the porch, to her. She stumbled backward, slamming the door shut and bolting it with trembling hands, her breath coming in shallow gasps. She pressed her back against the door, her heart pounding, the cold metal of the skillet clutched to her chest like a shield.

For a moment, there was only silence, the thick, suffocating quiet that filled the house like a fog. And then, the knocking began again—louder this time, as though something were pounding on the wood with a strength that defied human limits. The door rattled, the wood creaking under the force, and she could feel the vibrations reverberating through her bones.

"Go away!" she screamed, her voice breaking, but the knocking didn't stop. It grew louder, faster, until it was a relentless hammering that filled her mind, drowning out every thought, every instinct but one: survive.

She ran to the kitchen, grabbing her lantern from the counter, the warm glow flickering as she held it up like a lifeline. She backed toward the cellar door, her mind racing, searching for a way out, a place to hide. The cellar had a small, hidden hatch that led out to the forest; if she could just reach it, maybe she could escape, lose herself in the trees until whatever was outside gave up.

But as she fumbled with the lock, trying to pry it open, the pounding stopped. Silence fell once more, heavy and unnatural, as though the house were holding its breath. She turned slowly, the lantern trembling in her hands as she peered back toward the front door.

The figure was inside.

It stood in the doorway, its tall, thin form framed by the faint light of the moon filtering through the curtains. Its face was a mask of shadows, its eyes gleaming with that same unholy light, its mouth twisted into a grotesque, toothy smile. It took a step forward, its movements slow, deliberate, as though savoring the horror etched across her face.

Sarah felt her legs weaken, her body refusing to obey her commands, paralyzed by the sheer, overwhelming terror that gripped her. She stumbled back, her hand finding the cold, rough surface of the cellar door, her last hope slipping through her fingers as the figure moved closer.

In a final, desperate act, she raised the lantern, hurling it at the thing with all her strength. The glass shattered, flames bursting to life, casting eerie shadows across the room. For a moment, she thought she saw it flinch, its form twisting in the firelight, its face contorting with something that almost looked like anger.

But then, it stepped through the flames, unscathed, its eyes gleaming with a hungry, malevolent light. It was close now, so close she could feel its icy breath on her skin, smell the rancid stench of decay that clung to it like a second skin.

"Sarah..." it whispered, its voice a low, mocking hiss that sent chills down her spine. "There's no escaping me."

In a final, instinctive burst of fear, she turned, wrenching the cellar door open and stumbling down the stairs. She could hear it behind her, its footsteps slow but relentless, each one echoing in the small space like the tolling of a death bell.

She reached the bottom, her fingers scrabbling at the edge of the hatch. But as she lifted it, something cold wrapped around her ankle, yanking her back with a strength that sent her sprawling to the floor. She screamed, her voice echoing off the stone walls, but there was no one to hear her, no one to save her.

The last thing she saw was its face, twisted into a smile of pure malice, its eyes gleaming with satisfaction as it dragged her into the darkness. The light from the flames above flickered, casting shadows across the walls, but soon even that faded, leaving only the cold, silent dark.

The next morning, the farmhouse was empty. The front door hung open, the kitchen cold and lifeless. Only a faint trail of scorched wood led from the front door to the cellar, ending abruptly in a smudge of ash and the faint, lingering scent of smoke.

Ashwell fell silent once more, the fog thicker than ever, curling around the town like a predator licking its lips. And another house stood empty, another life swallowed by the shadows.

Chapter Six: Echoes of Fear

The townspeople of Ashwell were no strangers to bad luck, but these disappearances felt different. By now, no one could ignore the empty houses, the vacant workplaces, or the eerie quiet that seemed to thicken the very air they breathed. The four disappearances—Edna, Lou, Maddie, and Father Michael—were all people the town had leaned on, faces as familiar as their own. And then Sarah, the kindhearted soul who'd always been willing to lend a hand. Each day, her absence felt more like a ghostly presence, lingering in the shadows, haunting the town.

People began to gather in nervous clumps, their voices hushed but urgent, the unspoken dread drawing them together like moths to a dying flame. The Ashwell General Store became the main gathering place, its aisles packed with neighbors clutching cans of food, candles, anything that felt like it might ward off the dark that seemed to be closing in around them. Mr. Burke, the store's owner, stood behind the counter with an anxious frown, his gaze darting toward the windows every few seconds, as if expecting to see something—or someone—lurking outside.

"There's no use pretending anymore," Maggie, a mother of three, whispered to her neighbor as they clutched their shopping bags tight. "People don't just vanish into thin air. Not like this."

"Ain't natural," old Pete grumbled, his eyes darting suspiciously to the door. His weathered hands gripped his walking stick tighter than usual. "Something's been stalking this town. We all feel it."

"Maybe it's some kind of disease?" another voice suggested, though it wavered with doubt. "Something that makes people... wander off?"

But they all knew the truth, even if they couldn't bring themselves to say it. Disease didn't leave handprints smeared across bakery windows. Illness didn't knock on doors in the dead of night, or leave cryptic notes written in a spidery hand. This was something else, something that defied reason and made the hair on the back of their necks stand on end.

Huddled near the back of the store, a group of the town's younger men whispered plans. Caleb, Lou's nephew, had taken it upon himself to organize nightly patrols, men armed with flashlights, bats, whatever they could find. But as the days wore on and the nights grew longer, the patrols felt increasingly futile. They'd seen nothing in the shadows but their own fears, nothing out of place except for the cold fog that seemed to grow thicker with each passing hour.

"It's got to be someone, one of us," Caleb said one night, his voice low but intense as he addressed the small crowd in the store's back room. "People don't just vanish. Someone knows something. Someone has to."

The men around him shifted uncomfortably, their faces drawn and pale in the dim light. Trust had been the first casualty in this quiet war against an invisible enemy. Once-close friends now looked at each other with suspicion, neighbors keeping their distance, eyes wary, hearts guarded. The once-cozy town had become a collection of fearful individuals, each one afraid to reach out, each one wondering if the next knock on the door would be for them.

"I know it sounds crazy," Caleb continued, his voice barely a whisper, "but I swear I heard something last night. I was walking near the old church, just doing a round, and I heard it—this… whispering, like a hundred voices all at once, low and urgent, as if they were trying to tell me something."

A few of the men nodded, their faces tense with shared dread. Caleb wasn't the only one to report strange sounds—the whispers, footsteps that didn't match their own, low murmurs that seemed to come from nowhere and everywhere at once. The sounds had started subtly, barely more than a trick of the wind, but now, they seemed to follow the townspeople, dogging their every step, invading their homes, their dreams.

As the group dispersed, each man returned to his own home, a fortress locked up tight against the night. Curtains were drawn, doors were bolted, candles burned low into the night, as each household whispered its own private prayers for protection.

In the small, creaking house where Caleb and his younger sister lived alone since Lou's disappearance, the fear was tangible. He sat by the door, clutching his flashlight, his heart pounding with every tiny sound that drifted through the night. His sister, Mary, huddled on the couch, her wide eyes fixed on the darkened window.

"Do you think…" she began, her voice barely more than a whisper. "Do you think we're cursed?"

Caleb shook his head, but he didn't have the heart to give her any empty reassurance. His throat was tight with the same fear, a thick lump of dread that had lodged itself deep and refused to budge. "I don't know, Mary. I really don't."

In the meantime, a few houses down, Maggie paced back and forth in her small living room, her children fast asleep upstairs. She clutched a candle in her hand, its flickering flame casting shadows that danced along the walls, twisting into strange shapes. Every creak of the floorboards, every whisper of wind against the window, made her heart skip a beat.

"God help us," she murmured under her breath, clutching the candle tighter. "Please, God, help us."

But the nights grew darker, the fog thicker, and each morning, the town seemed emptier. People passed each other on the streets with quick nods, forced smiles that barely concealed the terror lurking behind their eyes. No one wanted to linger, to talk about what was happening. The unspoken fear bound them together as surely as any chain, and each one of them could feel the weight of it, heavy and cold, like a stone pressed against their chests.

By the end of the week, desperation had taken hold. The townsfolk gathered at the edge of the forest, the one place they'd never dared venture after dark. They stood in a tense huddle, lanterns raised, their faces etched with exhaustion and fear. They were done hiding, done waiting. They wanted answers.

"We should go out there," Caleb said, his voice hard with determination. "Whatever's doing this, it's hiding in those woods. We can't just sit around and wait for it to come for us."

There were murmurs of agreement, but others shook their heads, their faces tight with dread.

"You go in there, and you're as good as gone," Pete muttered, his gaze fixed on the dark line of trees. "That's where it wants us. It's been drawing us out, picking us off one by one. We're safer staying in town."

"Safe?" Caleb's laugh was bitter, sharp. "Is that what you'd call this? Locking ourselves away every night, praying it's not our turn? We're already prisoners here."

The crowd fell silent, the only sound the crackling of their lanterns. The trees loomed before them, dark and forbidding, and in the quiet, they could almost hear it—a faint whisper, like a distant echo, drifting from the depths of the forest.

"Maybe..." Maggie's voice broke the silence, her words soft, hesitant. "Maybe it's trying to tell us something. Maybe we've done something wrong, and this is our punishment."

There were nervous glances, murmurs of agreement and dissent. In the absence of answers, the townsfolk clung to what little sense they could make, desperate to understand, to find a reason for the nightmare that had overtaken their lives.

One by one, the lanterns began to dim as the crowd slowly dispersed, each person returning to their home, casting one last look at the dark forest before retreating into the safety of their walls.

That night, the fog was thicker than ever, pressing against the windows, seeping into every crack, every crevice. The whispers returned, louder this time, insistent and unrelenting, filling every corner of every home. Shadows danced along the walls, and doors rattled on their hinges, as though something on the other side were trying to force its way in.

As each family huddled together, the fear grew, sinking its claws deeper into their hearts. They could feel it now—the town itself closing in around them, a cage that grew smaller with each passing night. They were trapped, and they knew it, their once-safe haven transformed into a prison, with something dark and malevolent lurking just outside their doors, waiting, watching.

By morning, another house stood empty.

And Ashwell fell silent once more.

Chapter Seven: The Gathering Shadows

By now, the remaining townsfolk of Ashwell were caught in a waking nightmare. The once-cozy town, with its tightly knit community and familiar faces, had become a place of whispered dread and shared glances of fear. Each day, another face was missing from the morning gatherings, another house left abandoned, as if the town itself were slowly being hollowed out. The thick, ever-present fog wrapped around Ashwell like a noose, pulling tighter with each disappearance.

But today, they'd reached a breaking point. The town's council, a small group of elderly men and women who'd held their posts for decades, called for an emergency meeting in the town hall. It was a rare event, usually reserved for seasonal celebrations or the odd dispute over property lines. Today, however, there was nothing festive or mundane about the gathering.

They met in the dimly lit room, its high ceiling casting eerie shadows that seemed to stretch and shift with each flicker of the lamps. Everyone sat close, eyes darting to the corners of the hall, the darkness that now seemed to breathe and pulse with a life of its own. Caleb sat at the front, his jaw set in a hard line, his hands clenched into fists on the table before him. Around him were the last of Ashwell's stalwart residents, people who had survived every hardship life could throw at them. But this... whatever *this* was, it was beyond anything they'd ever known.

Mayor Avery, an older woman with sharp features and graying hair, stood at the head of the room, her face drawn and pale. She took a deep breath before she began, her voice steady but taut with the weight of what she was about to say.

"We are in a crisis," she said, her eyes scanning the weary, fearful faces before her. "What's happening here isn't normal—it isn't natural. People are disappearing, and this fog, this... darkness, it's changing our town, making it into something I don't recognize anymore. And I think we all know we can't wait any longer."

The crowd murmured in agreement, a tense undercurrent rippling through the room.

"We've been too silent, too afraid," she continued. "But fear is feeding whatever's lurking in this town. I feel it, don't you? It's as if our own fear is giving it strength."

Caleb's eyes flashed with determination as he spoke up, his voice rough but steady. "Then let's face it. We need to find out what's really going on, to look for the source of this... thing. Whatever it is, it's using the fog to hide itself, to take people without a trace. We can't let it keep picking us off."

"But how?" Maggie's voice trembled as she clutched her shawl tighter around her shoulders. "How do we fight something we can't see? Something that can just... slip into our homes like it owns the place?"

An uneasy silence settled over the room. The fog was no longer something they feared—it was something they hated. It had taken friends, family, neighbors. It had twisted their town into a haunted maze of whispers and shadows. And it would keep taking until there was nothing left of Ashwell.

An older man named Thomas, who'd lived in Ashwell his entire life, stood slowly, his voice thick with exhaustion and a raw edge of fear. "I remember, years ago, my grandmother used to talk about the old tales. Stories she'd heard from her own grandmother, about things that used to roam these mountains. They'd say the forest had eyes, spirits that watched over the town, bound to it by... by some old pact or curse, depending on who you asked."

Maggie shivered, her fingers nervously tracing the edge of her shawl. "But those were just stories, weren't they? My grandmother told me the same, but she was... well, she was old. Those tales were just to keep children in line."

"Maybe," Thomas replied, his gaze dark and distant. "But it feels like something's changed. Like something's woken up after lying dormant all these years. And it's angry."

Mayor Avery looked thoughtful, her eyes narrowing as she processed Thomas's words. "If there's any truth to those stories, then maybe there's a way to put this... *thing* to rest. But to do that, we need to know more. Does anyone else remember these tales? Something that could tell us what we're up against?"

The room fell silent, the weight of the question pressing down on them. It was Caleb who finally spoke, his voice low but filled with a grim resolve.

"There's one place we haven't searched yet," he said, his gaze fixed on the floor as though afraid to look up. "The forest. It's where the fog seems to come from, isn't it? It wraps around the trees before it reaches the town, as if it's spreading from a single point."

The suggestion sent a shiver through the crowd, murmurs of apprehension rising. Everyone in Ashwell knew the forest was off-limits after dark. For as long as they could remember, the trees held an unnatural stillness, a silence that felt watchful, almost resentful.

"You want us to go in there?" Maggie's voice was barely more than a whisper, her face drained of color.

"It might be our only chance," Caleb replied. "Whatever is taking us, it's hiding in there. If we go in together, maybe we can find it. Or at least figure out what we're dealing with."

Mayor Avery nodded slowly, her lips pressed into a thin line. "It's a risk, but we can't keep hiding. If we're to survive this, we need to be brave. We need to face it head-on, before it comes for the rest of us."

The group of townsfolk huddled closer, each one looking to the others for strength. They were scared, yes, but something stronger had taken root in their hearts now—a grim determination, a need to protect what was left of their lives. They couldn't let fear win. Not this time.

By the time the meeting ended, the plan was set. At dusk, they would enter the forest in a single group, bringing lanterns, flashlights, and whatever makeshift weapons they could find. They would march into the unknown together, guided by the dim hope that there might still be a way to break this curse, to rid Ashwell of the darkness that had sunk its claws into their lives.

As the sun began its descent, casting long shadows across the town, the townsfolk gathered at the edge of the forest. Each person clutched a lantern or flashlight, their faces grim and pale in the fading light. They stood shoulder to shoulder, staring into the depths of the forest, where the trees seemed to reach out like skeletal fingers, beckoning them forward.

Caleb took the first step, leading the group into the forest, his flashlight piercing the dense fog that hung low over the ground. The others followed, their footsteps muffled by the thick layer of fallen leaves, their breaths quick and shallow as they ventured deeper into the darkness.

The air grew colder as they moved further in, a biting chill that sank into their bones. The fog thickened around them, wrapping itself around their legs, their arms, clinging to them like wet shrouds. The trees closed in, their twisted branches casting shadows that danced and writhed in the dim light.

They walked in silence, the only sound the crunch of leaves underfoot and the occasional snap of a twig. The deeper they went, the more they felt it—a heavy, oppressive presence that seemed to pulse through the air, a dark energy that prickled their skin and set their nerves on edge.

And then, the whispers began.

They drifted through the trees, low and haunting, barely more than a murmur, like voices carried on the wind. Each word was unintelligible, but the tone was unmistakable—mocking, hungry, taunting them as they pressed forward. Some of the townsfolk gripped their lanterns tighter, their hands shaking, but they didn't stop. They had come this far; there was no turning back.

At last, they reached a clearing, a small circle of dead grass surrounded by towering trees. In the center stood an ancient stone altar, weathered and cracked, covered in strange symbols that seemed to writhe and twist in the firelight. The altar was dark with something that looked like dried blood, and around it were scattered fragments of bones, too large to be mistaken for animals.

The whispers grew louder, swirling around them like a chant, filling their ears with a sound that was almost musical in its cadence. And then, slowly, shadows began to take form around the altar—figures emerging from the fog, their faces obscured, their bodies twisting and shifting like smoke.

The townsfolk huddled together, their breaths coming in quick, shallow gasps as they watched the figures draw closer, their eyes gleaming with a malevolent light. The shadows moved slowly, deliberately, surrounding the group, their whispers merging into a single, mocking chorus.

One of the shadows leaned close, its face inches from Caleb's, its mouth stretched into a grin that seemed to split its face in two.

"Welcome," it whispered, its voice low and dripping with malice. "You've come so far. But this is where your journey ends."

And then, with a rush of cold, searing darkness, the figures descended.

Chapter Eight: The Descent

The shadows closed in, their forms shifting and writhing like smoke caught in an endless wind. The townsfolk of Ashwell stood frozen, their lanterns and flashlights illuminating nothing but the fog and the darkness that seemed to pulse and throb with life. Every instinct in their bodies screamed to run, but there was nowhere to go. The shadows circled them, each one grinning, mocking, savoring the fear that now radiated from their small, desperate group.

Caleb felt his breath hitch as he stared into the face of the figure before him, its eyes gleaming like coals, its mouth stretched wide in a grotesque, too-wide smile. He tried to move, to lift the bat in his hands, but his arms felt heavy, as though an unseen weight pressed down on him. The whispers grew louder, filling his mind, pressing against his thoughts until it felt like his very consciousness was being pried apart.

To his left, Maggie let out a strangled gasp, clutching her lantern to her chest as though it were a talisman. Her eyes were wide with terror, locked on the figure standing inches away from her, its head tilted as it regarded her with a cold, unblinking stare.

"Why... why are you doing this?" she whispered, her voice barely audible above the relentless chanting that filled the clearing.

The shadow before her leaned forward, its face inches from hers, and when it spoke, its voice was a low, mocking hiss that seemed to reverberate through her very bones.

"We are the silence that you left behind," it whispered. "The darkness that has always been here, waiting. Your fear has called to us, your secrets have fed us, and now, we are free."

With each word, the shadows seemed to grow stronger, their forms solidifying, becoming more distinct. Caleb saw them now—figures from his memory, twisted and distorted, their faces familiar but wrong, as though a child had drawn them with hands that trembled. He recognized Lou's face, his eyes hollow and empty, and Maddie's figure, her expression frozen in an unnatural smile that made his blood run cold.

The crowd began to murmur, their voices trembling, fear rippling through them like a shockwave. Some took a step back, only to find themselves pressed against the unyielding wall of darkness that had formed a perfect ring around them. The shadows laughed, a guttural, rasping sound that seemed to echo through the trees, mingling with the whispers that filled the air like a chorus of the damned.

Caleb took a shaky breath, his gaze fixed on the altar at the center of the clearing. The symbols carved into its surface seemed to pulse with a sickly light, shifting and writhing as though alive. The sight filled him with a sense of dread so profound it felt as though his heart were being crushed in his chest.

"This isn't just the fog," he murmured, his voice barely more than a breath. "This place... it's where it all began. Whatever's in these woods, it's been here for years. Waiting."

Thomas, the old man who had spoken of ancient stories, took a step forward, his eyes narrowed as he studied the altar. "I remember my grandmother telling me stories of an old pact, something binding Ashwell to these woods. She always said the forest was... hungry."

The shadow nearest to Thomas drifted closer, its form stretching, elongating as it leaned over him, its mouth twisted into a mocking grin. "Yes," it whispered, its voice a blend of glee and malice. "You have always known, even if you have long forgotten. We are bound to this land, and so are you. But now, the pact has broken. Now, we are free to feed."

The word hung in the air, thick and heavy, and Caleb felt a coldness settle over him, a chill that sank into his bones and refused to let go. He knew, in that moment, that there would be no escape. Whatever this *thing* was—whatever they were facing—it wasn't something that could be fought or reasoned with. It was ancient, relentless, and insatiable.

In a last, desperate attempt, Caleb raised his flashlight, pointing it at the nearest shadow, hoping the light might weaken it, force it back. But the beam passed through the figure as though it were smoke, illuminating nothing but the fog. The shadow laughed, a harsh, grating sound, and Caleb's hope withered, leaving only a hollow emptiness in its place.

"We can't fight them," he whispered, his voice shaking. "They're not... they're not real. They're shadows."

The townsfolk looked around, desperation mingling with terror as they realized the truth of his words. The shadows weren't physical, weren't something they could touch or strike. They were the darkness itself, the fear that had taken root in their hearts, twisted into something tangible, something alive.

One by one, the lanterns began to flicker, their flames sputtering as though struggling against an unseen force. Maggie's lantern was the first to go out, the flame snuffed out in an instant, leaving her standing in darkness. She let out a strangled cry, clutching her chest as the cold closed in around her, the shadows pressing closer, their whispers filling her ears.

"Please... please..." she whispered, tears streaming down her face as the figure before her leaned in, its eyes gleaming with a cold, merciless light.

The shadow smiled, its voice a soft, mocking murmur. "Your fear is delicious."

And with that, Maggie was gone, her scream cut off abruptly as the darkness swallowed her whole. The townsfolk gasped, horror and disbelief etched on their faces as they watched their friend disappear, her presence erased as though she had never existed.

The other shadows moved closer, their forms flickering and twisting, their voices merging into a cacophony of whispers and laughter. Caleb felt his own flashlight begin to sputter, the light flickering as though struggling against an unseen force. He clutched it tightly, his breath coming in short, desperate gasps as he tried to hold onto the last shred of light.

One by one, the remaining lanterns went out, each flame extinguished with a final, despairing flicker. The darkness closed in around them, thick and suffocating, pressing down on them with a weight that felt like the end of the world. The whispers grew louder, filling their minds, their souls, until there was nothing left but the cold, endless dark.

And then, there was silence.

Caleb blinked, his eyes adjusting to the sudden, oppressive blackness. He couldn't see anything, couldn't hear anything but the faint sound of his own breath, shallow and trembling. He reached out, his hand brushing against empty air, the space around him devoid of warmth, of life.

He was alone.

The weight of that realization hit him like a blow, and he felt his heart sink, a hollow, aching despair settling over him. He tried to call out, but his voice died in his throat, swallowed by the silence. The shadows had taken everyone. Maggie, Thomas, all the others—they were gone, consumed by the darkness, their lives erased as though they had never been.

Caleb took a shaky step forward, his hands outstretched as he stumbled through the dark, his mind racing, searching for something, anything that might explain what was happening. But there was only silence, only emptiness, stretching out before him like a vast, endless void.

And then, he heard it—a faint whisper, soft and mocking, drifting through the darkness.

"Caleb..."

He froze, his breath hitching as he recognized the voice. It was Lou's voice, but twisted, distorted, filled with a malice that sent a shiver down his spine. He tried to back away, but the darkness pressed in around him, holding him in place, trapping him in its cold, unyielding grip.

The voice grew louder, joined by others, each one familiar yet wrong, a chorus of voices he had known all his life, now twisted into something monstrous.

"Come to us, Caleb," they whispered, their voices mingling into a haunting melody. "You belong to us. Ashwell belongs to us."

He felt something cold brush against his shoulder, a touch that sent a jolt of terror through him. He tried to move, to break free, but the darkness held him fast, its grip unrelenting, suffocating. He could feel it seeping into him, filling his mind, his soul, until there was nothing left but the shadows.

In his final moments, as the last remnants of his consciousness faded, Caleb understood the truth. The darkness, the whispers, the shadows—they were Ashwell. They were the fear, the secrets, the anger that had festered in the town for generations, twisted into something alive, something hungry.

And now, they had him too.

When dawn broke over Ashwell, the fog remained thick, curling around the empty streets, the silent houses. The town was quiet, devoid of life, as though it had been abandoned long ago. No one remained to tell the story, no one left to remember the lives that had once filled its streets.

Ashwell had fallen silent, its secrets buried in the fog, its people swallowed by the darkness that had claimed them.

Chapter Nine: The Watchful Fog

The sun rose over Ashwell, casting a faint, reluctant light over the town. But the fog remained, clinging to the streets and curling around the empty houses like an ever-present shroud. It lingered, a patient witness, as though holding on to the last traces of what had once been. The streets were silent, the houses vacant, their windows staring out into the morning light like empty eyes.

Days turned into weeks, yet no one ventured into Ashwell. Those who lived in nearby towns whispered about the place, shaking their heads as they spoke of strange noises and shadows seen from afar. Some claimed they heard voices echoing in the night—whispers that drifted through the trees, carrying names and memories from a town that no longer existed.

Only the remnants remained: a weathered sign at the town's entrance, half-obscured by weeds and moss, the words "Welcome to Ashwell" barely legible beneath layers of grime. The trees stood taller now, their branches reaching over the road as if trying to shield the town from prying eyes, to hide the secrets that lay within.

And in the dead of night, when the fog was thickest, shadows moved through the town. Figures without faces, voices without bodies, they wandered the empty streets, replaying fragments of lives long gone. A woman's laugh echoed faintly from the bakery's window, a man's rough voice murmured from the garage, the faint clink of a priest's rosary whispered from the church.

Then, one crisp autumn morning, a stranger appeared at the town's edge. A young man, backpack slung over his shoulder, eyes squinting as he looked into the fog-shrouded streets. He stepped over the old boundary, his feet crunching on leaves as he walked down the empty road. He paused by the church, his gaze drifting to the closed doors, an odd sense of familiarity tugging at him.

"What happened here?" he murmured to himself, his voice breaking the silence.

The fog seemed to thicken around him, as though listening, considering. He shivered, feeling the chill of the morning air seep into his skin, the weight of the silence pressing down on him. For a moment, he thought he saw movement—a shadow slipping between the trees, a flicker of light from a distant window. But when he looked again, there was nothing. Just the quiet, the stillness, the thick, unrelenting fog.

Unnerved, he turned and walked back down the road, glancing over his shoulder as he crossed the town's boundary. The fog parted briefly, just long enough for him to catch a glimpse of the empty streets, the silent houses, and the shadows that watched him from the edges of the trees.

As he left, the fog closed around Ashwell once more, sealing it away like a memory forgotten, a secret buried. And in that stillness, the shadows resumed their restless wandering, waiting patiently, bound to the fog and the land, watching... always watching.

Ashwell was gone, swallowed by the fog, a ghost town left to haunt itself.

But the fog never truly left.

And somewhere, in a distant whisper carried by the wind, the town waited, patient as ever, for another soul brave—or foolish—enough to wander into its embrace.

Don't miss out!

Visit the website below and you can sign up to receive emails whenever Catherine J Rosser publishes a new book. There's no charge and no obligation.

https://books2read.com/r/B-A-FGQOC-NXZDF

BOOKS 2 READ

Connecting independent readers to independent writers.

Did you love *Ashwell: Shadows in the Fog*? Then you should read *The Thistle Queen*[1] by Catherine J Rosser!

In the cursed forest of Thrysseldown, where shadows whisper and thorns grow thicker than hope, the Thistle Queen reigns. Once a guardian of the land, her heart was corrupted by forbidden love and betrayal, casting an ancient curse that turned the forest into a realm of twisted magic. Now, the forest thrives on fear, its paths shifting and dark creatures lurking in every shadow.

Elowen, a humble gardener with an extraordinary connection to the earth, stumbles upon a long-forgotten

1. https://books2read.com/u/bayO1L

2. https://books2read.com/u/bayO1L

secret—the truth of the Thistle Queen's curse. Alongside Rook, a roguish thief with a haunted past, and Periwinkle, a cursed fae prince in the form of a fox, Elowen embarks on a perilous quest to restore the forest and free its people from the Queen's relentless grasp.

As they journey deeper into the heart of Thrysseldown, battling ancient magic and facing their darkest fears, they unravel the tragic history of the Queen and her once-sacred bond to the forest. But breaking the curse comes with a price, and not everyone will survive the trials of the forest. In a land where light and darkness blur, and sacrifice is inevitable, Elowen must decide how far she is willing to go to restore balance and confront the Queen who was once the forest's savior.

The Thistle Queen is a dark fairytale of magic, sacrifice, and redemption, set in a world where the forest holds its own secrets, and even the deepest love can turn to ruin.

Read more at https://catherinejrosser.com/.

Also by Catherine J Rosser

The Eternal Magic Series
The Magic Within

The Isles of Fate Series
The Crimson Raven: A Tale of Captain Poppie O'Malley
The Siren's Call: A Tale of Love and Treachery on the High Seas
Winds of Fortune

The Keeper of Ages
The Eternal Circle
The Shattered Veil
The Ascendant Path

Standalone
Beyond the Horizon
Echoes in the Abyss

Haven Falls

The Fractured Mind

The Next Chapter: Embracing Midlife with Purpose, Peace, and Possibility

The Thistle Queen

Dream Interpretation: A Journey Through the Mind's Mirror

Ashwell: Shadows in the Fog

Witch's Brew: A Spellbinding Guide to Magical Cooking and Ethical Kitchen Witchery

Watch for more at https://catherinejrosser.com/.

About the Author

Catherine J. Rosser is a fantasy author who weaves together myth, magic, and unforgettable journeys. Known for her vivid storytelling and rich characters, she brings epic worlds to life with themes of destiny and self-discovery. When not writing, Catherine draws inspiration from nature, channeling its beauty into her imaginative tales.

Read more at https://catherinejrosser.com/.